Jessie
the Lyrics
Fairy

To Madeleine and Jude Boddice with lots of love

Special thanks to Sue Mongredien

No part of this publication may be reproduced, stored in a retrieval
system, or transmitted in any form or by any means, electronic,
mechanical, photocopying, recording, or otherwise, without written
permission of the publisher. For information regarding permission,
write to Rainbow Magic Limited c/o HIT Entertainment,
830 South Greenville Avenue, Allen, TX 75002-3320.

ISBN 978-0-545-48474-9

Previously published as *Pop Star Fairies #1: Jessie the Lyrics Fairy*
by Orchard U.K. in 2012.

All rights reserved. Published by Scholastic Inc., 557 Broadway, New
York, NY 10012, by arrangement with Rainbow Magic Limited.

12 11 10 9 8 7 6 5 4 3 2 1   13 14 15 16 17 18/0

Printed in the U.S.A.   40

This edition first printing, March 2013

Jessie
the Lyrics
Fairy

by Daisy Meadows

SCHOLASTIC INC.

Jack Frost's Ice Castle

Campsite

Girls' tent

Main Stage

Karaoke tent

Café

The Harbor

Rainspell

Island

It's about time for the world to see
The legend I was born to be.
The prince of pop, a dazzling star,
My fans will flock from near and far.

But superstar fame is hard to get
Unless I help myself, I bet.
I need a plan, a cunning trick
To make my stage act super-slick.

Seven magic clefs I'll steal —
They'll give me true superstar appeal.
I'll sing and dance, I'll dazzle and shine,
And superstar glory will be mine!

Contents

Off to the Island

"Rainspell Island, here we come!" cheered Kirsty Tate, pointing ahead to the green island that had just come into view. She and her best friend, Rachel Walker, were on the deck of a ferry heading to the island, which was a very special place. Not only was it where the girls had first met, it was also the place

where they'd had their very first fairy
adventure.

"Almost there," said Rachel. "I can't
wait to see The Angels again, can you?"

"It's going to be awesome," Kirsty
replied. The Angels were the girls' favorite
band. They were performing at the five-
day Rainspell Island Music Festival!
Kirsty and Rachel were going to camp
out at the festival with Rachel's parents.

"Music, fashion, fun — we're
going to have the
best time ever!"
Rachel smiled.

"And what
would make it
even better,"
Kirsty said,
lowering her

voice, "is if we could meet some new fairies, too."

The girls exchanged a secret smile.

It was thanks to the fairies that they were here at all. One Christmas, they'd won a competition to meet The Angels and had ended up helping Destiny the Rock Star Fairy find her missing magical objects. To thank the girls for their help in making their Christmas concert a success, The Angels had invited them to the summer music festival as their special guests.

"We will be arriving at Rainspell Island soon," a voice said over the speaker just then. "Thank you for traveling with us today."

The island was really close now, and the girls could see a huge stage set up in one of Rainspell's lush green fields.

There were tents of all sizes and campers everywhere, some flying colorful flags.

"That must be the festival!" Rachel said excitedly. "Oh, I have such a good feeling about this, Kirsty. I know we're going to have a fabulous time!"

The girls left the ferry with Mr. and Mrs. Walker and made their way toward the busy festival site. They could hear loud music and smell hot dogs, onion rings, and cotton candy. Then Kirsty gasped. "There are The Angels!" she cried. "Look — they're over by the main entrance!"

There was a long line to get into the festival, but as soon as the three Angels spotted Kirsty and Rachel, they waved them over. "Hey — welcome to Rainspell!" Serena said with a smile. "It's good to see you again."

"You, too," the two friends said together.

"We have your backstage passes here," Lexy said, holding up laminated passes on pink ribbons. "With these, you'll be able to skip the line and go straight in with us."

"We can even show you Star Village, if you'd like," Emilia suggested. "There's a lot of really cool stuff going on there."

"Thank you — that's so nice," Mrs. Walker said, looping her pass around her neck. She looked almost as excited as the girls, Rachel noticed with a grin.

Together,
they all
walked to
Star Village,
a collection
of tents where
you could try
all kinds of fun
things: learn musical instruments and
dance routines, experiment with hair and
makeup, and even design funky costumes
just like real stars.

"We'll leave you here to check it all
out," Emilia said after a while. "We
need to do our sound check now."

"The campsite is the next field over,
when you want to set up," Serena said
after she noticed the bulky tent bag that
Mr. Walker was carrying.

"I hope you'll come and see us perform later," Lexy added. "We're opening the festival this afternoon."

To the girls' delight, the three singers broke into one of their greatest hits, "Key to My Heart." They sang the chorus in harmony:

"You're always there to hold my hand,
You stand by me, you understand.
When I'm with you I feel so glad,
The truest friend I ever had.
I know we two will never part,
And that's the real key to my heart!"

"I love that song!" Kirsty smiled. "It makes me think about being best friends with Rachel."

"Me, too!" Rachel said.

The Angels gave them high fives.

"That's great," Lexy said. "See you later!"

Kirsty and Rachel grinned as the band walked away. "I can't believe we're actually

friends with The Angels, Rachel." Kirsty sighed. "They are *so* cool!"

"I know," Rachel said dreamily. "It's almost as amazing as being friends with the fairies," she added in a whisper. "We're definitely the luckiest girls in the world!"

A Meeting with Destiny

When they reached the campsite, Kirsty and Rachel helped Mr. and Mrs. Walker put up the tent. The girls would be sharing one of the sleeping areas, so they blew up their air mattresses and unrolled their sleeping bags. It was going to be cozy in there at night, Kirsty thought, putting her pajamas under her pillow with a smile.

Rachel's parents were just hammering in the last tent stakes when Rachel spotted a sparkly piece of material at the bottom of the tent bag. "What's this?" she asked, picking it up.

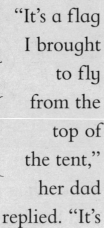

"It's a flag I brought to fly from the top of the tent," her dad replied. "It's so colorful, it'll make it easy for you girls to see it through the crowd and find your way back to the tent."

"Cool," said Rachel, unrolling the flag. As she did, something glittery fell out . . . and then soared up into the air. It

was Destiny the Rock
Star Fairy!

Kirsty ran over
and waved
happily at their
pretty fairy
friend. She
didn't dare
to speak,
though, in
case Rachel's
parents overheard.
The girls knew that they
had to keep the fairies a secret from
everyone else.

She and Rachel motioned for Destiny
to follow them to the back of the tent,
where they could talk without having to
worry about being overheard.

"Hello!" Kirsty said. "What a nice surprise. Have you come to hang out with the stars at the festival?"

Destiny smiled. Her magic made sure that concerts went perfectly in the human 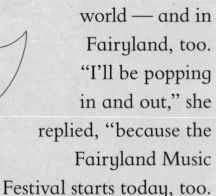 world — and in Fairyland, too. "I'll be popping in and out," she replied, "because the Fairyland Music Festival starts today, too. In fact, I was wondering if you two would like to come to Fairyland with me and watch the rehearsal?"

"Yes, please!" Rachel said at once. Her heart thumped at the thought of going back to Fairyland. It was the most exciting place ever!

Even better, time stood still in the human world while they were in Fairyland, so nobody would know that the girls had been gone.

"I was hoping you'd say that," Destiny exclaimed. With a wave of her wand, a fountain of sparkling fairy dust swirled all around the girls. In the blink of an eye, they were whisked off the ground. Everything blurred before their eyes in a whirlwind of rainbow colors.

When the glittery whirlwind finally

cleared, Rachel and Kirsty found
themselves in a Fairyland meadow —
and they were fairies! Kirsty couldn't
resist fluttering her wings and floating
up into the air. Being able to fly was so
wonderful!

"Oh, wow, is that a fairy campsite?"
Rachel asked, gazing at the field in front
of them. They could see a lot of colorful
toadstool-shaped huts and tents.

"I bet that's Danielle the Daisy Fairy's tent," Kirsty said with a giggle, pointing to a tent with a colorful yellow and white flower design.

"Yes, this is the festival camping area," Destiny said, fluttering into the air. "Let's see how everyone is doing backstage."

Kirsty and Rachel flew after their friend, looking down at the festival site with interest. They could see the Music Fairies

setting up their instruments onstage, the Dance Fairies stretching and warming up, and the Petal Fairies decorating the equipment with garlands of colorful flowers. Everyone seemed very excited.

Backstage, Destiny headed straight for a group of seven fairies who were deep in conversation. "Kirsty, Rachel, these are my very good friends the Superstar Fairies," she said, and introduced them all. There was Jessie the Lyrics Fairy, Adele the Voice Fairy, Vanessa the Choreography Fairy, Miley the Stylist Fairy, Frankie the Makeup Fairy, Alyssa the Star-spotter Fairy, and Cassie the Concert Fairy.

To Kirsty's surprise, the Superstar Fairies seemed awfully distracted. "Hi," they said, but their smiles didn't last long. Maybe they were just nervous about performing?

"Good luck! I'm sure the rehearsal will be fine," Destiny said breezily. "Let's take our seats in the audience," she added to Rachel and Kirsty.

As the girls turned to leave, Rachel couldn't help noticing that the Superstar Fairies immediately huddled together and began whispering anxiously. "We'll just have to hope for

the best," she heard Jessie say. How strange!

Destiny led them to their seats near Queen Titania and King Oberon, who waved and smiled.
A cheerful song started  playing, and the Superstar Fairies came onstage to begin the rehearsal!

Rachel listened eagerly. She was sure that fairy pop music would be awesome! But then the fairies started singing, and Rachel almost immediately changed her mind.

"Oh, no," Kirsty murmured, as Cassie and Jessie both forgot the lyrics of the first verse.

"Oops," Rachel whispered, wincing as Vanessa and Alyssa got their dance routine wrong and bumped into each other.

Frankie's dangly earrings fell out and Adele's dress ripped . . . and *all* of them were singing out of tune!

Destiny looked horrified. "This is a disaster!" she whispered.

"What's wrong?" Kirsty asked. She was sure the Superstar Fairies weren't usually this bad.

"I think they must have forgotten their clefs," Destiny whispered back. "A clef is a symbol used when writing down music, and all the Superstar Fairies have magical G clef necklaces. When they wear them, it helps keep pop music wonderful in both your world and ours. Without the necklaces, performances can go very wrong — like this one." She scratched her head. "But I don't understand. They *always* wear their magic clefs. How could they have forgotten *today*, of all days?"

Rachel's heart sank. "So without their clefs, performances in the human world will go wrong, too?" she asked. "I hope they remember to put them back on soon!"

Just then, a cold breeze swept through the audience. Icicles appeared around the stage, and a white layer of frost covered the ground. Kirsty felt goose bumps

prickle across her arms, and she glanced at Rachel in alarm.

"Oh, no — is Jack Frost here?" She gulped.

Before anyone could reply, Jack Frost and his goblins strutted onto the stage. Jack Frost was dressed like a rock star, and Destiny gasped in dismay as she saw that seven necklaces were hanging around his neck — each with a music clef of a different color on it.

"Oh, no," Destiny cried. "So the Superstar Fairies didn't *forget* their magical clefs. Jack Frost must have stolen them!"

Memory Mayhem!

Queen Titania had also noticed that
Jack Frost was wearing the magic clef
necklaces. She quickly rose to her feet.
"Those don't belong to you," she called
out. "Please give them back to the
Superstar Fairies."

A sly smile appeared on Jack Frost's
cold, pointy face. "No way," he said.

"Not now that I know what they do."
He played a series of chords on his
guitar, the notes ringing out perfectly
around the stage. The goblins clapped,
and Jack Frost bowed.

"I've definitely got the Frost Factor,"
he cackled, "and
I'm going to
use these
magic
clefs to
make
me the
biggest
star that
the Rainspell
Island Music
Festival has ever seen. Nothing's going to
stop me now!"

A flash of icy blue magic lit up the stage and, before anyone could react, Jack Frost and his goblins had disappeared. With a quick glance, Rachel could see that Destiny had turned pale and all of the Superstar Fairies looked very upset.

"Your Majesties, Kirsty and I are staying at the Rainspell Island Music Festival," said Rachel. "We'll try our best to get the magic clefs back for you while we're there."

"Thank you," King Oberon replied, looking serious. "That's very kind. Jessie, maybe you can take the girls back to the human world and help them."

"Of course," said Jessie at once, jumping lightly off the stage. She had black hair and big dangly hoop earrings. Over her dark leggings, she was wearing a long, colorful shirt. Over that, she had on a T-shirt with lots of shiny bottle caps sewn on one shoulder.

"Good luck," Destiny said. "And please do your best. Without those clefs, I'm afraid pop music is in big trouble."

"We'll try our hardest," Jessie promised. "Let's go!"

She waved her wand and a flurry of orange sparkles swirled around the three of them, lifting them into a glittery whirlwind. The anxious faces of their fairy friends vanished before Kirsty's and Rachel's eyes as they were swept away.

Moments later they were back on Rainspell Island, and they were still fairies. "Let's fly around and look for Jack Frost," Jessie suggested. "But remember to stay out of sight. There are so many people here, we can't let anyone see us!"

The three fairies zoomed high above the crowds, searching for any signs of Jack Frost or his goblins causing trouble. They flew into the backstage area — a large, airy tent lined with comfortable couches, special practice areas where the performers could rehearse, and tables full of sandwiches and cookies.

Kirsty felt tingly with excitement as she spotted her favorite boy band, A-OK, practicing their harmonies. She saw other pop stars there, too. "Sasha Sharp, Groove Gang, Dakota May, Jacob Bright . . ." she said, pointing them out to Rachel. "Wow!"

"No one looks very happy, though," Rachel said as one of the A-OK boys put his head in his hands.

Dakota May came to a stop in the middle of her song and let out a wail. "I forgot the words *again*!" she cried.

"They keep forgetting their song lyrics," Kirsty realized.

"Oh, no," Jessie groaned. "It's because Jack Frost has my clef. When I'm wearing it, it helps superstars compose great lyrics — and remember them, too!"

"Look, there are The Angels," Rachel said, spotting them rehearsing in a far corner. "Let's see if they're having better luck."

Unfortunately, as they flew closer, it became obvious that The Angels were also struggling.

"You're always there to . . . make my tea . . ." Serena sang. Then she looked confused. "No, that's not right."

"You're always there to . . . hold my bags . . ." Emilia tried next, frowning. "What *is* that line again?"

"We have to find my magic clef as soon as we can," Jessie said. "The Angels are supposed to be opening the festival in half an hour, and they can't remember the first line of their biggest hit. This could go horribly wrong!"

"Well, there's no sign of Jack Frost in here," Kirsty said. "Let's try looking somewhere else."

The three fairies flew out of the backstage tent and around the festival site. There were lots of people having fun in Star Village, enjoying the sunshine and setting out picnic lunches, but Jack Frost and the goblins were not in sight.

Rachel was just starting to wonder if he was even at the festival at all, when she noticed a big crowd pouring into the karaoke tent. "We could try looking in there," she suggested.

Jessie and Kirsty agreed, and they flew closer. Someone inside was rapping! As they approached the tent, the three fairies realized the same thing at the same time: the rapper's lyrics were coming out perfectly.

"He's the only person we've heard at this festival who is getting the words right," Jessie said. "I bet that means he's near my magic clef!"

All Change

Kirsty, Rachel, and Jessie immediately flew over the crowd and into the karaoke tent to investigate. Inside, there were small karaoke booths set up with microphones and TV screens. All of the booths were empty except for one, where the rapper stood, surrounded by a huge crowd. He wore a shiny green jacket and a hat with a large brim that hid his face from view. As he finished the rap, he bowed low, and the audience cheered.

The rapper swaggered around. "Thanks," he said into the microphone. "Glad you liked it. That was a song by Jax Tempo, my hero! He's the only rapper in the whole world who's better than me." He patted his throat. "Gotta protect this voice of mine now, so that was the last song. Later, guys!"

Rachel's eyes widened as he patted his throat and she noticed a gleam of orange beneath his fingers. Immediately, she nudged her friends.

"Look!" she whispered. "Did you see what he has around his neck?"

Jessie peered excitedly down at the rapper. "It's my clef!" she exclaimed. "Jack Frost must have split the clefs up and given them to his goblins to hide!"

"Goblins are too vain not to use the clefs themselves!" Kirsty giggled. "But there are so many people around. How are we going to get near him without anyone seeing us?"

The three friends tried to think of a solution. "If we can somehow get him to take it off . . ." Jessie murmured, scratching her head.

Rachel smiled. "I have an idea," she said. "We'll suggest that he needs a style change. Like this . . ." She whispered her plan to the other two.

"Let's fly into an empty booth, and I'll work some magic on you two," Jessie said after Rachel had finished. "Quick," she added as the goblin gave a last wave to his fans and began heading toward the exit. "Before we lose sight of him."

The three fairies swooped down into a booth. When nobody was looking, Jessie waved her wand, releasing a sparkling stream of fairy magic. A second later, both Kirsty and Rachel were back to their usual size — but now they each wore a disguise! Kirsty was wearing a pantsuit with a badge that read STAR SPOTTER.

Rachel had an official festival hat on her head, and held a clipboard in her hands.

"So you're a music agent, and I'm a festival organizer," Rachel said, giggling. "Come on, let's try it. I'll meet you backstage. Good luck!"

She hurried off, and Jessie flew up to one of the speakers high in the ceiling of the tent. Once she was in place, she gave Kirsty a thumbs-up. Kirsty smiled back, took a deep breath, and walked toward the goblin. She hoped this plan would work!

Superstar!

"Hi, I'm Crystal Gold, agent to the stars,"
Kirsty told the goblin. "I'm always on
the lookout for amazing new talent —
and I think you're it."

The goblin looked delighted and struck
a pose. "Well, I *am* pretty good, it's true,"
he replied boastfully.

"The Angels keep forgetting their song lyrics, and the festival people are worried they won't be able to perform their best," Kirsty went on. "So I'd like to suggest you as their replacement. What do you think — are you up to appearing on the main stage as our opening act?"

"Oh, yeah!" the goblin said, nodding. "Finally, my chance to shine in the spotlight!"

Kirsty scratched her ear — the secret signal she and Jessie had agreed on — and saw a tiny stream of sparkles flash above the speaker. Then a voice boomed out. "Attention, please. Could our opening act proceed to the main stage now. Thank you."

Jessie had used fairy magic to disguise her voice. She sounded just like an announcer over a loudspeaker — and by the look of excitement on the goblin's face, she had been very convincing.

"What are we waiting for?" he whooped. "Let's go!"

He raced eagerly toward the main stage.
Kirsty held her jacket pocket open so that
Jessie could dive inside and hide there.
Then Kirsty ran after the goblin. She
took him to the wings of the main stage
and used her backstage pass to get them
both inside. As they'd planned,
Rachel was there to
meet them.
"Hmm,"
Rachel
said,
critically
looking
the goblin
up and
down.
"I'm not
sure. . . ."

The goblin's face drooped. "What do you mean?" he asked.

"I don't know if you've got the star quality we're looking for," Rachel told him. "You don't look quite right."

"He can change," Kirsty said, elbowing the goblin. "Can't you? You could wear something different."

"Yes, of course!" the goblin replied, clearly desperate to get on the main stage at any cost. "I'll do anything!"

"OK, well, for starters, the shiny jacket and the hat need to go," Rachel ordered.

The goblin obediently took them off.

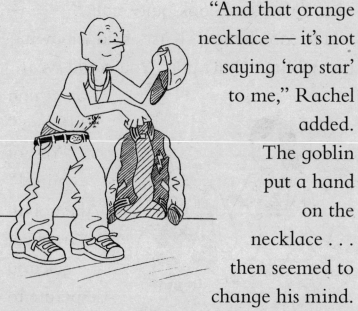

"And that orange necklace — it's not saying 'rap star' to me," Rachel added.

The goblin put a hand on the necklace . . . then seemed to change his mind. "No," he said stubbornly. "The necklace stays."

Rachel hesitated. Oh, no! That wasn't part of the plan. She was just wondering

what to say next when Kirsty had a
stroke of genius.

"Don't worry," Kirsty said, patting the
goblin's arm. "As your new agent, I'll
sort this out for you. Wait here." She
dashed behind a rack of costumes and
whispered to Jessie, "Can you use your
magic to make something that the
goblin will want
to wear around
his neck?"

Jessie
grinned and
leaned out
of Kirsty's
pocket to
wave her
wand.

There was a swirl of orange sparkles,

and then a chunky gold chain appeared in Kirsty's hand. A large medallion that read SUPERSTAR dangled from it.

"Perfect!" Kirsty said with a giggle, and she went to find the goblin. "Here," she said. "This will look *much* cooler than that flimsy little necklace."

The goblin's eyes lit up. "Superstar — yes, that's me!" he agreed. He grabbed the gold chain, then ripped off Jessie's clef necklace and tossed it aside.

Kirsty reached out and caught the necklace, then passed it to Jessie. The fairy immediately shrank the necklace down to fairy-size. As she fastened it around her neck, the clef began to shine. The three friends beamed. They'd done it!

The goblin, meanwhile, was practicing
his act and hadn't noticed any of this!
Unfortunately, now that he wasn't
wearing Jessie's clef necklace, his rapping
wasn't quite as smooth as it had been
before.

Kirsty and Rachel were just wondering
how they were going to break the news

to the goblin that he wasn't going to open the festival after all, when they heard a booming voice. "Who's that rapping *my* words?"

A tall man was striding in their direction, wearing a shiny blue suit, an enormous pair of sunglasses, and an ice-white hat.

"Jax Tempo!" The goblin rapper gulped, looking terrified. He turned and fled without another word.

"Wait — I thought he was your hero!"

Kirsty called in surprise. "Don't you want to meet him?"

Jax Tempo walked past them, toward the rehearsal area. "Nobody's a better rapper than I am," they heard him brag. "Soon I'll be the biggest superstar in the *world*!"

There seemed to be something familiar about him, Rachel thought. She couldn't put her finger on what it was! But before she could think about it anymore, she heard an announcement over the backstage speaker.

"Could The Angels make their way to the main stage, please. The show will begin in two minutes."

Kirsty turned anxiously to Jessie. "I'm glad The Angels will be able to remember their lyrics now that you have your necklace back, but what about all the other superstar magic? Will they be able to remember their dance steps without Vanessa's magic, and sing well without Adele's powers?"

"Don't worry," Jessie smiled. "My clef has enough superstar magic to ensure that the whole performance will go smoothly, as long as I stay close to the stage and focus all my strength on the band.

Thanks so much
for helping
me get my
necklace
back!"

With a wave
of her wand,
Jessie changed the
girls back into their normal clothes.

"Good-bye, Jessie," Rachel said, smiling
at the little fairy. "That was fun!"

"Good-bye," Kirsty said as Jessie
darted toward the stage, like a spark of
fire. Then the girls hurried around to the
front of the stage and waited excitedly. A
large crowd had gathered, and everyone
cheered as the first chords of "Key to
My Heart" sounded. The three Angels
ran onstage.

The Angels looked nervous at first, but as they launched into the song and got the words and harmonies absolutely perfect, they started to relax and smile.

Rachel and Kirsty were dancing and singing along in the front row. "Look, there's Jessie,"  Rachel whispered, pointing to where they could see a tiny dot of twinkling light high above the stage. From the way the dot was wiggling around, Rachel was sure Jessie was dancing, too.

When the song ended, the audience clapped and cheered. Then everyone gasped as a puff of rainbow-colored glitter swirled across the stage. "Just like magic," Rachel heard a girl nearby say, and she exchanged a smile with

Kirsty. Both friends were pretty certain that the glitter *had* been magic — a burst of fabulous fairy magic from Jessie!

"That was awesome!" Kirsty sighed happily. "I'm so glad we helped Jessie find her clef in time."

"Me, too," Rachel said. "Now we just need to track down the six other magic clefs to make sure the rest of the festival is as good."

"One thing's for sure," Kirsty said. "It's going to be another exciting vacation — with fairies, music, and adventures. I can't think of anything better!"

Jessie has her magic clef back.
Now it's time for Kirsty and Rachel to help

Adele
the Voice Fairy!

Join their next adventure
in this special sneak peek. . . .

A Picnic Surprise

"What a fantastic place for a picnic!" Rachel Walker exclaimed, her face breaking into a huge smile.

She and her best friend, Kirsty Tate, were standing on a grassy hill above the site where the Rainspell Island Music Festival was taking place. The girls were camping there for five fun-filled days.

Below them, the two friends could see an enormous stage surrounded by lighting and sound equipment. Close by was Star Village, where festival-goers were able to try being superstars themselves. The village had a karaoke tent as well as a small stage for dance classes. There were other areas where people could try out hairstyles and makeup, and even design their own stage costumes. There were lots of stalls and food tents, too, and a campsite for the festival-goers where Rachel, Kirsty, and Rachel's parents were staying.

"OK, girls," called a voice behind them. "The picnic's ready."

Rachel and Kirsty spun around eagerly. Their friends Serena, Lexy, and Emilia, otherwise known as the famous

singing group The Angels, were sitting
on a fluffy pink picnic blanket, smiling
up at them. Rachel's and Kirsty's eyes
grew wide as they saw the plates and
bowls of delicious food surrounding the
three girls. Yum!

"Oh, this looks so glamorous!" Kirsty
sighed as she and Rachel joined The
Angels on the picnic blanket. There
were fancy triangular sandwiches
and a crystal bowl filled with ripe red
strawberries next to another bowl of
whipped cream. A jug of freshly made
lemonade with floating ice cubes and
slices of lemon stood in the cool shade of
a nearby tree. . . .

These activities are magical!
Play dress-up, send friendship notes, and much more!

RAINBOW magic™

SPECIAL EDITION

Three Books in Each One—
More Rainbow Magic Fun!

Joy the Summer Vacation Fairy
Holly the Christmas Fairy
Kylie the Carnival Fairy
Stella the Star Fairy
Shannon the Ocean Fairy
Trixie the Halloween Fairy
Gabriella the Snow Kingdom Fairy
Juliet the Valentine Fairy
Mia the Bridesmaid Fairy
Flora the Dress-Up Fairy
Paige the Christmas Play Fairy
Emma the Easter Fairy
Cara the Camp Fairy
Destiny the Rock Star Fairy
Belle the Birthday Fairy
Olympia the Games Fairy
Selena the Sleepover Fairy
Cheryl the Christmas Tree Fairy
Florence the Friendship Fairy
Lindsay the Luck Fairy

■ SCHOLASTIC

scholastic.com
rainbowmagiconline.com

HIT entertainment

RMSPECIAL10

RAINBOW magic™

There's Magic in Every Series!

The Rainbow Fairies
The Weather Fairies
The Jewel Fairies
The Pet Fairies
The Fun Day Fairies
The Petal Fairies
The Dance Fairies
The Music Fairies
The Sports Fairies
The Party Fairies
The Ocean Fairies
The Night Fairies
The Magical Animal Fairies
The Princess Fairies
The Superstar Fairies

Read them all!

■ SCHOLASTIC

scholastic.com
rainbowmagiconline.com

Prospect Heights Public Library
12 N. Elm Street
Prospect Heights, IL 60070
www.phpl.info

HiT entertainment

RMFAIR